Hey Jack! Books

First American Edition 2014
Kane Miller, A Division of EDC Publishing

Text copyright © 2013 Sally Rippin
Illustration copyright © 2013 Stephanie Spartels
Logo and design copyright © 2013 Hardie Grant Egmont

First published in Australia in 2013 by Hardie Grant Egmont

For information contact:
Kane Miller, A Division of EDC Publishing
P.O. Box 470663
Tulsa, OK 74147-0663
www.kanemiller.com
www.edcpub.com
www.usbornebooksandmore.com

Library of Congress Control Number: 2013944869

Printed and bound in the United States of America
3 4 5 6 7 8 9 10
ISBN: 978-1-61067-261-0

The Best Party Ever

By Sally Rippin

Illustrated by Stephanie Spartels

Kane Miller
A DIVISION OF EDC PUBLISHING

Huge grin

Feels like running
and jumping

Buzzy feeling
in toes

Bouncy Mood

Chapter One

This is Jack. Jack is
in a bouncy mood.
It's his birthday party
today! He has invited
the whole class.

Jack's house isn't big enough for twenty-three kids. So this year he is having his party at a play center.

Jack wakes up feeling very **excited**. He runs downstairs to the kitchen. "It's my birthday party today!" he shouts.

Jack's mom and dad are

eating breakfast.

3

"You still have four hours before your party," says his mom.

"Come and have some breakfast. We'll get ready in a little while."

After breakfast, Jack says, "I'm going to Billie's house." Four hours is too long to wait by himself.

4

Billie is Jack's best friend.

She lives next door.

Jack **squeezes**

through the hole in

the fence into Billie's

backyard.

He runs up to the back

door and knocks on

the glass.

Billie's mom comes to
the door. She is still in
her bathrobe.

"I'm sorry, Jack,"

she says. "Billie is sick!

She has been throwing

up all night. Something

she ate must have upset

her tummy. She won't

be able to go to your

party today."

"Oh no!" says Jack.

"You can go upstairs and visit her," says Billie's mom. "She'll be happy to see you."

Jack runs up the stairs two at a time. He **bursts** into Billie's room. She is sitting up in bed with a book.

"You're not coming to my party?" says Jack.

"I know!" says Billie miserably. "My mom won't let me. She says I'm too sick."

Jack sits down on Billie's bed. He feels very disappointed. "But it won't be fun without you!" he says.

Billie smiles. "Thanks, Jack. But you'll still have fun. Not too much, I hope!" she jokes. "Save me some cake, won't you?"

"Of course I will," he says. "I wish you could come, too."

Jack knows his party won't be the same without Billie. What fun is a party without your **best friend**?

Chapter Two

Jack arrives at the
play center with his
mom and dad.
One by one, the kids
from Jack's class arrive.

They are all very **excited**.

"This is awesome, Jack!" shouts Sam. He gives Jack a present. Then he runs over to the tunnel slide. Benny and Alex are already sliding down at top speed.

"Wow, cool place!" says Tracey. She gives Jack a present, too. Then she runs over to the ball pit. She and Ella sink into the colored balls.

Jack feels very proud. No one in his class has ever had a party as cool as this!

Soon the play center
is very busy and very
noisy. Jack feels a little
bit nervous. It feels
strange not to have
Billie around.

When Billie is with
him, Jack feels brave
enough to do anything!

19

Just then, Benny runs over. He has a grin as big as a whale. "Hey, Jack!" he yells. "Come and play! Alex is It!"

Jack feels a little bubble of excitement in his tummy. "OK," he says. "Let's go!"

20

Jack follows Benny.
They run over to the
play equipment. Alex is
chasing Mika and Ella.

Alex tags Ella on the shoulder. "You're It!" he shouts.

Ella runs straight toward Jack. But Jack is too **fast**. He swings up onto the play equipment to get away. Then he slides down the long tunnel slide.

22

When he pops out at the bottom, Ella is waiting for him. She tags him before he can get away.

"Jack's It!" she shouts and quickly climbs up a ladder.

Jack laughs and runs after Tracey. She **jumps** into the ball pit and balls fly everywhere!

Jack and his friends play tag until his mom calls them for cake.

Everybody is laughing and puffing so hard that they can hardly sing the birthday song.

"This is the best party ever!" says Ella. She takes a **huge** bite of chocolate cake.

"Sure is!" says Alex. "Thanks so much for inviting us."

"Yeah," Tracey agrees. "It's so great you could invite the whole class.

Everyone is here!"
She helps herself to
another sandwich.

"There's one piece of
cake left," Jack's mom
says. "Anyone want
seconds?"

"Me, please!" says Sam.
He licks his lips.
"It's super yummy!"

Everyone laughs.

Especially Jack.

He looks at his

classmates and smiles.

Ella is right, he thinks.

This is the best party ever!

Chapter Three

That afternoon when
Jack gets home, he
runs straight over to
Billie's house.
She is still in bed.

She looks very lonely and very bored.

"I had the best party, Billie!" he says happily. He **bounces** up and down on her bed. "The play center was amazing. You should have seen the ball pit! We had so much fun.

And everyone *loved* the birthday cake."

Billie smiles. "Did you save me some?"

"Oh," says Jack. "I forgot!"

"What about a goody bag?" Billie asks.

Jack feels his cheeks get hot. "Sorry," he says. "Benny took an extra one."

"What about the presents?" Billie says. "Did you wait for me to open them?"

Jack bites his lip and
shakes his head. "No.
I opened them already."

Billie frowns. She pulls her blanket up to her chin. "You didn't miss me at all! You didn't save me one thing!"

Jack feels hurt that Billie is so **cross** with him. "Well, it's not my fault!" he says. "You didn't come to my party!"

"I couldn't, could I?"
Billie shouts. "I was sick!"

"Well you don't have
to shout at me!"
Jack says.

He storms out of
Billie's room.
Then he stomps all
the way home.

By the time he is back
in his bedroom, Jack
already feels bad.

Billie is right, he thinks. *I did forget her. I was having such a good time that I forgot my best friend!*

Jack tries to think of something that will make Billie feel better.

He looks over at his box of Lego. Suddenly he has an idea. He tips all the colored pieces onto his desk. Then he begins to build.

He builds ladders and slides and climbing frames. He even builds a ball pit with tiny colored balls.

It takes him a long time. But Jack is happy with his work. It looks just like the play center.

Last of all, he chooses lots of tiny Lego characters. They will be all the people in his class.

And this time he is very careful not to forget Billie.

Collect them all!